The Petal Fairies

For Ella Gavra,
with lots of love

Special thanks to
Sue Mongredien

ORCHARD BOOKS
338 Euston Road, London NW1 3BH
Orchard Books Australia
Level 17/207 Kent Street, Sydney, NSW 2000
A Paperback Original

First published in 2007 by Orchard Books

HiT entertainment

A CIP catalogue record for this book is available from the British Library.

ISBN 978 1 84616 464 4

10

Printed in Great Britain

Orchard Books is a division of Hachette Children's Books

www.orchardbooks.co.uk

Ella
the Rose
Fairy

by Daisy Meadows

ORCHARD

The
Fairyland
Palace

Fairy Garden

Blossom
Hall

Leafley Village

Visitors' Centre

I need the magic petals' powers,
To give my castle garden flowers.
And so I use my magic well
To work against the fairies' spell.

From my wand ice magic flies,
Frosty bolt through fairy skies.
And this crafty spell I weave
To bring the petals back to me.

Contents

Roses Need Rescuing

"Here we are, the Chaney Palace Flower Show," Mr Walker said, looking at the steady stream of people heading towards the entrance. He smiled at his daughter, Rachel, and her best friend, Kirsty Tate. "What a flowery week we've had!"

"We love flowers!" Rachel said,

giving Kirsty a secret smile.

"Especially since we met the Petal Fairies," Kirsty agreed in a whisper.

The girls linked arms as they followed their parents into the field where the flower show was taking place. The two families had been spending the Easter holidays together, and the girls had been helping the Petal Fairies find their missing magic petals. They had found six petals so far, but there was still one left to find – the Rose Petal.

"What's in here?" Mr Tate wondered aloud, as they approached a large marquee. "Ah, the rose tent," he said, reading the sign on the entrance.

Kirsty and Rachel exchanged excited glances; maybe the missing Rose Petal would be inside? A group of people were leaving the tent as the Tates and the Walkers approached.

"Very disappointing," a man said gloomily. "I've never seen such unhealthy flowers!"

The Tates and the Walkers stepped inside the tent and Rachel saw that the man was right. All the roses were drooping, their petals faded and withered.

11

Rachel bit her lip. She and Kirsty knew why the roses weren't doing well. The Petal Fairies' magic petals helped flowers grow in Fairyland and around the world. But the bad fairy, Jack Frost, had sent his goblin servants to steal the petals so that he could use their magic to make flowers bloom around his ice castle. When the Petal Fairies had tried to stop the goblins, the magic petals had been blasted into the human world. Now that the petals weren't in their proper place in Fairyland, flowers everywhere were wilting and dying.

"Let's go and see some of the gardens instead," Mr Walker suggested, looking sadly at the drooping roses.

Rachel turned to Kirsty as they left. "The other flowers should be beautiful because we've already found the other petals and sent them back to  Fairyland," she whispered.

"But we've got to rescue these roses!" Kirsty nodded. "I bet all the dark pink flowers in the show are dying," she added.

The Petal Fairies had told the girls that each magic petal looked after its own type of flower, and other flowers of a particular colour. The Rose Petal helped roses and all dark pink flowers to grow.

"We've got to find the petal before

13

the goblins do," Rachel whispered.

"This is their last chance to take a petal back to Jack Frost. I'm sure they'll be trying extra hard to find this one!"

The girls knew that the goblins were trying to find the fairy petals for their master. And to make things even more difficult for Kirsty and Rachel, Jack Frost had given his goblins a wand full of his own icy magic, to use against them.

As the two families wandered down

the path, Kirsty could see that the
display gardens were set out in one long
row, with a separate area for each.

"What a lovely Japanese garden!" her
mum exclaimed, stopping at the first
garden. "Look at that bamboo."

"And isn't the fountain pretty?"
Mrs Walker put in.

Rachel couldn't concentrate on the
Japanese garden, though, because she'd
just seen the sign outside the next one.
'Fairy Garden' it read.

She nudged Kirsty. "Look!"
The fairy garden had
a wrought iron gate at
its entrance, and was
filled with flowers in
all colours of the
rainbow. There
was a winding
path, made of
glittering stones,
and a bench
where you could
relax and look
for fairies.

"Mum, can we go
into the fairy garden?"
Kirsty asked.

Mrs Tate smiled. "Of
course," she said. "Why don't we split

up and meet you later? Shall we say one hour from now in the tea tent?"

"Perfect!" Kirsty said, as her parents waved goodbye and walked on to look at the other gardens. "Come on, Rachel!"

"The Petal Fairies would love it here." Kirsty said, pushing open the gate and walking in. "Definitely," Rachel agreed, following her friend. Then, suddenly, she stiffened.

"Kirsty, look!"

Kirsty followed Rachel's pointing
finger to see a large, healthy-looking
rose bush absolutely covered with
dark pink flowers in the back corner
of the garden. "The magic petal must
be near that bush," Kirsty gasped,
"otherwise the roses wouldn't be
looking so beautiful!"

"Yes," Rachel said happily. "So—
Oh!" She broke off as she noticed that
the rose bush was rustling. "It's moving!"

Kirsty's smile vanished. "What if
it's goblins?"

Luckily, nobody
else was in the
garden, so
the girls
were able
to tiptoe
down the
path and
over to the
rustling roses.
Cautiously, they
peeped round the
side of the bush.

Seven naughty goblins were pulling all the roses off the bush! They were wearing boys' clothes, clearly hoping to blend in with the other visitors at the show, and they were trying to sort through the rose petals to find the magic petal.

"Ugh, pink!" the girls heard one goblin complain. "Such a horrible colour!"

"Green is much better," another agreed.

Kirsty looked at Rachel anxiously, wondering how they were going to find the petal before the goblins.

Just then a silvery voice came from behind them. "Hello, girls! I love your pink outfits."

Kirsty and Rachel swung round to see a smiling fairy fluttering in mid-air!

Maze Magic

"Ella!" Kirsty cried, edging away from the rose bush, so that she could speak to the fairy without being overheard.

"We're so glad to see you!" Rachel added.

Ella the Rose Fairy had long, dark, wavy hair and wore a pink floaty dress with a sash around the middle.

As she opened her mouth to speak to the girls, a jubilant cry came from behind the rose bush.

Kirsty, Rachel and Ella all peeped through the leaves in alarm. To their dismay, they saw that one of the

goblins was holding out his cupped hands...and the magic Rose Petal was lying in them! Rachel thought quickly. "Ella, could you use your fairy magic to make the petal float out of his hands — and over here, to us?" she suggested.

"Yes!" Ella replied eagerly, pointing her wand at the bush.

A stream of sparkles swirled from the tip of her wand and over the thorny branches.

The girls watched in glee as they saw the sparkles surround the magic petal, lift it up into the air and carry it back over the bush. The plan was working!

But then a green hand appeared and snatched the petal back.

"You're staying with us!" the girls heard a goblin say.

"What's going on?" another asked – and then three goblin faces appeared around the side of the bush.

"We might have guessed," sneered one. "It's those silly girls with a silly fairy."

"Come for the petal, did you?" another gloated. "Bad luck!"

"Please may I have it?" Ella asked. "It *is* mine, you know!"

"Not any more, it isn't!" the goblin holding it laughed. "It's ours. And we're giving it straight to Jack Frost. He'll be very pleased with us!"

Just then, one of the goblins burst out laughing, pointing at the girls and Ella. "Look at them, all in yucky pink!" he guffawed.

"Pink stinks!" another yelled.
"We're off!"

And with that, the goblins all rushed
out of the back of the fairy garden,
taking the Rose Petal with them.

"After them!" Kirsty cried.

Ella swooped to hide under Rachel's
hair as the girls raced after the goblins.
The goblins ran past an English
cottage garden, then a rockery, before
turning off into a maze
of hedges.

Kirsty just had
time to glimpse the
sign as she
followed. It read,
'Chaney Court
Hedge Maze. Can
you find the statue in the middle?'

The goblins scattered, each charging off down different paths.

"Which one has the petal?" Rachel asked in despair, not sure which goblin to chase.

"I'll turn you both into fairies," Ella decided. "Then we can fly and hopefully spot the petal from above!"

In a shower of pink sparkles, Kirsty and Rachel found themselves shrinking to fairy size.

Gorgeous, shimmery wings appeared on their backs, and they immediately zoomed up above the maze. "I can see three goblins," Kirsty said, pointing them out. "Oh, and there's another…" "There's one in the middle, by the statue," Rachel added. "And look what he's holding!" "My petal!" Ella cried joyfully.

The three friends zoomed towards the statue. "Ella, if you turn us back to our normal size, Rachel and I can try to get your petal back from him," Kirsty suggested.

Ella lifted her wand, but Rachel stopped her.

"Hold on," she said, pointing down at the maze. "The other goblins are nearly at the centre too, and I don't think we'll be able to get the petal away from all of them." Ella nodded. "Let me make the maze a little bit more difficult for them," she said with a cheeky grin.

30

She zipped over and sprinkled some fairy dust over the one path that led to the centre of the maze. Instantly, a thick new section of hedge appeared, blocking the way to the little clearing where the statue stood.

The goblin who was already by the statue stopped and stared at the new hedge. "Hey! I'm trapped!" he yelled.

"And his friends won't be able to come to his rescue!" Kirsty realised with a giggle. "Perfect, Ella!"

Rachel grinned. "Now let's get that petal!" she cried.

Pink Lightning

Rachel and Kirsty swooped down to the centre of the maze, and Ella turned them back into girls with another wave of her wand.

The goblin was surprised to see them appear in front of him. "Help! Those girls have found me!" he shouted to his friends in alarm.

Kirsty grinned. "You can shout all you like, but they won't be able to help you."

Rachel held out her hand. "You might as well give us the petal now," she told him, "because you're trapped in here with us!"

The goblin hid the petal behind his back. "I'm not giving it to you," he said stubbornly.

"Hang on! We're coming!" another goblin's voice called from somewhere over the hedge.

"It's no use," the goblin with the petal shouted back. "They've got me stuck here with their pesky fairy magic!"

"Well, those fairies should know by now that we have our own magic!" came an answering shout, and the girls jumped because the voice sounded quite close behind them.

There was a rustling sound and Rachel and Kirsty turned to see the goblins' wand poking through the hedge.

Before the girls could do or say anything, one of the goblins started chanting a spell.

"This will stop those girls, I think. Lightning bolts, zap all things pink!" he cried from the other side of the hedge.

Kirsty looked down at her top in horror. She was wearing pink – and so were Rachel and Ella. They were all about to get blasted by the goblins' icy magic! "Hide!" yelled Kirsty, ducking behind the statue as lightning bolts fizzed straight through the hedge towards her.

CRASH! One bolt hit the statue – and to the girls' great surprise, it turned the statue bright pink!

CRASH! Another bolt struck the goblin with the petal.

Rachel and Kirsty stared at him in shock. He had turned pink, right before their eyes!

Ella gave a tinkling laugh. "It's because of the way the goblin said the spell," she explained. "When he said 'Lightning bolts zap all things pink', he meant for lightning to hit everything that's pink – but instead, it's turning things pink!"

The goblin with the petal seemed quite unaware of his colour change. "It hasn't worked!" he shouted through the hedge. "The lightning missed the pesky pink fairy and her friends!"

Three goblins peered through the hedge – and immediately burst into fits of laughter. "Hey, pink suits you!" one of them teased.

"What?" demanded the goblin with

the petal. He looked down at himself
and gasped in horror. "I'm pink!"
he wailed.

"It's definitely your colour," Rachel
chuckled.

"Very you," Ella agreed, spluttering
with laughter.

"It's not funny!" the pink goblin
snapped, stamping his foot. "Turn me
green again right now!"

Once the goblins on the other side
of the hedge had managed to stop
laughing, the wand was poked through
the branches again, and the girls heard
another goblin clear his throat for
a second spell.

"Oh no, you don't!" Kirsty cried, darting forward and snatching the wand right out of his hand.

"Hey!" came an indignant shout. "Give that back!"

"No chance," Kirsty replied happily. But then she gulped in alarm, because, suddenly, the magic stretch of hedge that Ella had conjured up vanished in a burst of pink sparkles, and all the other goblins charged into the centre of the maze!

A Frosty Atmosphere

Ella quickly turned the girls back into fairies, so they could zoom up into the air and escape the goblins. The goblins' wand that Kirsty was holding became fairy-sized, too.

"Hey – give our wand back!" one of the goblins shouted.

"Jack Frost will be mad if we come

back without it," another fretted,
jumping up to try and catch the girls.

"Sorry, guys," Rachel grinned. "But—"

She broke off as she
spotted a girl in
a lilac T-shirt
drawing closer to the
centre of the maze.

"Oh, no!" Rachel
gulped. "Look!"

"We mustn't
let her see the
goblins!" Ella cried.

Kirsty's mind raced,
and then she remembered she had
a magic wand in her hand. She
quickly pointed it down at the goblins,
and tried to think up a spell. "Whisk
this magic far away, back to Jack

Frost's hideaway!" she declared.

A magical wind began to blow around the goblins, sweeping them up into the air. But then Kirsty felt a cold wind tugging at her, too.

"Oh, no!" Ella exclaimed. "We're part of 'this magic' too. We've been caught up in the spell!"

Kirsty gulped as the wind grew even stronger. "You mean..." she began.

Ella nodded. "We're on our way to Jack Frost!"

Everything blurred before the girls' eyes, as they were whisked up in the magical whirlwind with the goblins.

When the whirl of magic finally died away, the girls and Ella saw that they were hovering in mid-air, a short distance from Jack Frost's ice castle. Below them, the goblins were lying in a heap of tangled arms and legs in the snow.

Jack Frost turned in surprise, from where he'd been feeding his snow geese on the pond.

"Oh, it's you lot!" he snapped. "What have you got for me?" Kirsty, Rachel and Ella quickly fluttered behind a nearby tree, hoping Jack Frost wouldn't notice them. Luckily, his eye was drawn straight to the goblin at the bottom of the heap, who was still bright pink. "What on earth...?" Jack Frost spluttered. "What have you been doing?"

"It wasn't my fault!" the pink goblin moaned. "And look what I've brought you!" he added proudly, wriggling until he could get his hand out from under the other goblins. He was still clutching the Rose Petal between his fingers.

"At last! A magic petal of my own!" Jack Frost cried triumphantly. "Now I will have all the flowers I want growing around my castle!"

48

Poor Ella could hardly bear to look. "If Jack Frost gets his hands on my petal, I might never get it back again," she whispered miserably.

"What if Kirsty and I distract him?" Rachel suggested. "Then you fly over and grab the petal while he's not looking!"

"OK!" Ella said, brightening. "Let's try it."

Ella set off towards the petal, while the girls flew out into the open, behind Jack Frost.

Kirsty saw that Jack Frost was just bending down to grab the petal.

"Hey, Jack Frost!" she called quickly. "Aren't you wondering where your wand is?"

Jack Frost turned in surprise, and glared when he saw Kirsty and Rachel.

"We've got it!" Rachel added.

"And we're going to cast a spell on you!" Kirsty cried.

"How did you get my wand?" Jack Frost bellowed furiously.

He immediately strode away from the

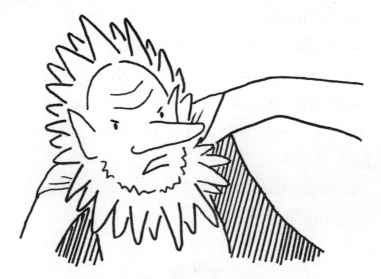

goblins, towards the girls. "I'll have that back, thank you," he snapped. He stared hard at the wand, then lifted his hand up and muttered a magic word. Instantly, the wand flew from Kirsty's grasp back to its master.

With a horrible grin, Jack Frost pointed the wand at the girls. "Maybe this will teach you to stop meddling!" he told them. And then, as he muttered a spell, a freezing lightning bolt came shooting out of the wand – straight towards Rachel and Kirsty.

Frozen Flowers

"Hide!" shouted Rachel, and she and Kirsty dodged behind the tree trunk. Neither of them could see Ella now, but they both really hoped she'd been able to grab her petal.

Kirsty peeped around to look for Ella, and then drew back in alarm as two more lightning bolts flashed past. She and Rachel clung to each other.

"What are we going to do?" Kirsty asked, as lightning bolts whistled past

the tree, only just missing the girls. "I don't know," Rachel replied. "Sooner or later one of these is going to hit us!" But as the girls looked at each other in panic, Kirsty suddenly saw a stream of pink fairy dust sparkling in the sky above them. As she watched, the fairy dust began to turn into brightly coloured flowers which rained down to the ground in between the girls and Jack Frost. More and more flowers formed in the sky, and floated down, creating a curtain of falling flowers. And Jack Frost's lightning bolts were bouncing right off the flowers, no longer able to get anywhere near the girls.

"The flowers are acting like a shield," Kirsty realised.

"It must be the Petal Fairies' petal magic!" Rachel cried in delight.

"And, look, there they are!" Kirsty exclaimed, pointing to where Ella was hovering in mid-air, along with the other Petal Fairies: Tia, Louise, Charlotte, Danielle, Olivia and Pippa. All of them were beaming and waving at Kirsty and Rachel.

"Ella must have rescued her petal when we distracted Jack Frost," Rachel laughed. "And now all the Petal Fairies have come to rescue us!"

Kirsty nodded happily. "Look!" she said, pointing to the curtain of flowers. "When the icy lightning bolts hit the magic wall, they freeze the falling flowers. Aren't they pretty?"

Rachel grinned. "Yes, and Jack Frost obviously thinks so too!" she pointed out, because Jack Frost was no longer hurling lightning bolts at the girls. Instead, he was now bending down and scooping up armfuls of the frozen flowers.

"Hey, you lot!" he shouted to his goblins. "Come and help me collect these. They're just the thing for decorating my castle gardens!"

The goblins, who'd untangled themselves by now, ran over to help. "Look at these frozen sunflowers!" one of them whooped. "They'll look good over here," he added, planting them in the ground. Being frozen, they stood up straight and sparkled prettily with frost.

"These tulips are nice," another goblin sighed. "I might take a bunch home to my mum."

Ella and the other Petal Fairies flew down to join the girls.

"Thank you for saving us from Jack Frost," Kirsty said.

Ella laughed. "We're the ones who should be thanking you," she told the girls. "You've been brilliant – again!"

Tia smiled. "Let's leave Jack Frost to his frozen flowers," she suggested, taking Kirsty by the hand.

Louise came over and took Rachel's hands. "Yes, let's go," she said.

"Where to?" Kirsty asked, feeling excited.

Olivia smiled. "To the Fairyland palace, of course!" she said. "King Oberon and Queen Titania are waiting to see you!"

A New Friend

The seven Petal Fairies led Kirsty and
Rachel away from Jack Frost's castle to
the beautiful gardens outside the
Fairyland palace, where the girls saw
the fairy King and Queen waiting for
them. They were standing next to
a pool that glittered in the sunlight.

"Well done!" Queen Titania said

warmly as the girls landed. "We
watched everything
in the seeing pool,
here. Rachel and
Kirsty, you
have done
a marvellous
job, helping
the fairies to get
all their magic
petals back."

"Yes, we couldn't have done it
without them," Charlotte the
Sunflower Fairy beamed.

"And now that Jack Frost has his
everlasting ice flowers, he won't
trouble our Petal Fairies again,"
the King added. He shook his head,
looking exasperated. "If he'd just

come and asked us for help in the
first place, instead of trying to steal
the magic petals, none of this would
have happened."

Ella waved her wand over Kirsty and
Rachel and, to their surprise, garlands
of rainbow-coloured flowers appeared
around their necks.

"Thank you!" Rachel exclaimed.
"They're beautiful!"

"It's a pleasure," Ella replied. "They're just a little something to remember us Petal Fairies by."

The Queen lifted her wand. "I'm afraid it's time for me to send you back to the human world now," she said. "Oh, yes, we're supposed to be meeting our parents soon," Kirsty agreed.

"Goodbye, girls," Ella said, giving Rachel and Kirsty a last hug. "And thanks again!"

"Goodbye," the two girls chorused.

The Queen waved her wand over them and they were whisked away

from Fairyland in a blur of colours.
Seconds later, they found themselves
back in the maze, and at their
normal size.

"It's strange being here without
Ella or the goblins," Kirsty said,
looking around.

Rachel nodded. "Much quieter!"
she laughed.

"And look," Kirsty said, "our flower
garlands have turned into necklaces.
Aren't they pretty?"

Rachel saw that Kirsty was right – they were both wearing necklaces, made of glittering, flower-shaped beads. There were seven different beads that matched the colours of the magic petals. And the necklaces were beautiful!

Just then, a girl with a lilac T-shirt walked into the centre of the maze. Of course! Kirsty thought. It's the girl who was about to reach the

middle, when we were whisked
away to Fairyland.

"Hi," said the girl. "My name's
Arabella Diers. This maze is hard, isn't
it? It's taken me ages to get here!"

"I'm Rachel," Rachel replied. She
didn't know what to say about the
maze. After all, she and Kirsty had
flown to the middle. They hadn't
actually had to find their way through
the maze at all. Suddenly, she realised
that they didn't have a clue how to
get out!

"It is hard,"
Kirsty was saying.
"In fact, we
can't remember
the way out.
Can you?"

Arabella nodded. "I think so," she said. "Follow me!" As she turned to lead the way out, she caught sight of the girls' necklaces. "Ooh! They're pretty," she commented.

It didn't take the three girls long to get out of the maze.

"There you are!" Arabella said proudly as they reached the exit.

"Thank you," Kirsty said. Impulsively, she pulled off her fairy necklace and handed it to Arabella.

"Here – have this," she said. "To say thanks for helping us." Arabella's face lit up.

"Oh, thank you!"
she breathed, looking
starry-eyed
with delight.
Rachel and
Kirsty grinned.

"That was nice of you,"
Rachel said, taking her own necklace
off as Arabella walked away. "If you
like, we could try and make my
necklace into anklets. Then we can
have one each."

Suddenly, she gasped as the necklace
started to shimmer with
a sparkly pink light. As
the girls watched, the
necklace split apart and
transformed itself into
two pretty anklets.

Kirsty stared at Rachel, open-mouthed. "How did you do that?" she gasped.

Rachel was just as surprised as Kirsty. "I didn't do anything! The fairies must have been watching over us," she said with a smile. "Thank you, Petal Fairies!" She handed an anklet to Kirsty, and both girls fastened them around their ankles.

"We'd better go and meet our parents," Rachel remembered. "Come on!"

The girls rushed over to the tea tent, just in time to see their parents sitting down by a beautiful, flowering rose bush. "Aren't these fantastic?" Mrs Walker said to Rachel and Kirsty, sniffing one of the blooms.

"Yes, and funnily enough, when we passed the rose tent a minute ago, all the roses were looking much better!" Mr Tate put in.

The girls exchanged happy glances.

Now that the Rose Petal was back in Fairyland, it was working its special magic all over the world again. Roses and dark pink flowers everywhere would be growing healthily once more.

Mr Walker smiled at the girls. "Did you have fun?" he asked.

"Yes, thanks," Rachel told him. "The maze was really good."

"Yes, it was great fun!" Kirsty added. The two girls grinned at one another. They both loved their fairy adventures. Being friends with the fairies made everything fun!

Now Rachel and Kirsty
must help...

Bethany the Ballet Fairy

Read on for a sneak peek...

"I'm *really* looking forward to this!" exclaimed Rachel Walker to her best friend, Kirsty Tate. "I *love* ballet."

"Me, too," Kirsty agreed, raising her voice above the noise of the train as it rattled over a bumpy bit of track. "I've never seen *Swan Lake* before."

"I've heard that this is a fantastic production," Kirsty's mum said. "The scenery is supposed to be gorgeous."

"Well, let's hope it keeps Dad awake!" Kirsty laughed, glancing at her dad who was fast asleep in the corner seat. "I'm so pleased you could come, Rachel. Wasn't it lucky that your school finished for half-term the day before ours? You wouldn't have been here in time to come with us otherwise."

Rachel nodded. Because their families lived quite a long way apart, she was staying with Kirsty for the whole week of the half-term holiday.

"We'll be in London soon," said Mrs Tate, as the train drew into a station. "This is the last stop before we get there."

Kirsty stared out of the window as the train slowed. Suddenly her attention was caught by a flash of icy blue streaking past the window. Puzzled, Kirsty leaned forward for a closer look.

Read Bethany the Ballet Fairy to find out what adventures are in store for Kirsty and Rachel!

Meet the fairies, play games
and get sneak peeks at
the latest books!

www.rainbowmagicbooks.co.uk

There's fairy fun for everyone on
our wonderful website.
You'll find great activities, competitions, stories and
fairy profiles, and also a special newsletter.

Get 30% off all Rainbow Magic books at

www.rainbowmagicbooks.co.uk

Enter the code RAINBOW at the checkout.
Offer ends 31 December 2012.

Offer valid in United Kingdom and Republic of Ireland only.

Win Rainbow Magic Goodies!

There are lots of Rainbow Magic fairies, and we want to know
which one is your favourite! Send us a picture of her and tell
us in thirty words why she is your favourite and why you like
Rainbow Magic books. Each month we will put the entries into
a draw and select one winner to receive a Rainbow Magic
Sparkly T-shirt and Goody Bag!

Send your entry on a postcard to Rainbow Magic Competition,
Orchard Books, 338 Euston Road, London NW1 3BH.
Australian readers should email: childrens.books@hachette.com.au
New Zealand readers should write to Rainbow Magic Competition,
4 Whetu Place, Mairangi Bay, Auckland NZ.
Don't forget to include your name and address.
Only one entry per child.

Good luck!

Meet the
Dance Fairies

Jack Frost has stolen the Dance Fairies' magic ribbons! Kirsty and Rachel must get them back, or dance everywhere will be ruined.

www.rainbowmagicbooks.co.uk